HOMER AND THE HOUSE NEXT DOOR

by Robin Pulver

illustrated by Arnie Levin

Four Winds Press ❖ *New York*

Maxwell Macmillan Canada   *Toronto*   Maxwell Macmillan International   *New York   Oxford   Singapore   Sydney*

Four Winds Press
Macmillan Publishing Company
866 Third Avenue
New York, NY 10022
Maxwell Macmillan Canada, Inc.
1200 Eglinton Avenue East
Suite 200
Don Mills, Ontario M3C 3N1
Macmillan Publishing Company is part of the
Maxwell Communication Group of Companies.
First edition
Printed in Singapore on recycled paper

10   9   8   7   6   5   4   3   2   1

The text of this book is set in Leawood Book ITC.
The illustrations are rendered in pen and ink and dyes.
Book design by Christy Hale

Library of Congress Cataloging-in-Publication Data
Pulver, Robin.
Homer and the house next door / by Robin Pulver ; illustrated by
Arnie Levin.—1st ed.
p.   cm.
Summary: Homer the dog tries to discourage his master from selling
their house and moving.
ISBN 0-02-775457-X
[1. Dogs—Fiction.   2. Moving, Household—Fiction.]   I. Levin,
Arnie, ill.   II. Title.
PZ7.P97325Hq   1994
[E]—dc20   93-3477

Disgusted!

That's how Homer felt when his good friend Ms. Gallivant moved out of the house next door. He hid when he was supposed to say good-bye. But when she drove away, he ran to watch. A strange sign stood in Ms. Gallivant's front yard. Moving is dumb, thought Homer. Nobody should move.

Homer's master, Hank, put his arm around Homer. "How could Ms. Gallivant leave such a wonderful house?" Hank said. "It's the best house on the block."

Homer missed Ms. Gallivant.

He missed the biscuits she baked for him and the way she knew just where to scratch him when he itched. He missed the tennis balls she threw for him to fetch as she hung her laundry out to dry.

Homer worried about who might move into Ms. Gallivant's house. He loved her yard. On hot days, he liked to lie in the shade of her huge willow tree. Would the new neighbors let him do that?

Would the new neighbors mind when Homer chased the wild rabbits that lived by the hedge? Ms. Gallivant knew that Homer would never hurt them. She understood that the chase was just a game.

Ms. Gallivant always let Homer take the shortcut through her yard to play with the Robinson children next door. Would the new neighbors let him do that?

A postcard arrived from Ms. Gallivant.
Hank read it to Homer.

Homer sneezed when he sniffed the postcard. It wasn't as good as Ms. Gallivant's biscuits.

Hank sighed. "What do you think, Homer?" he said. "Are we in a rut, too? Would a move be good for us?"

Homer sat up and barked NO.

Then Hank said, "Oh, heck, I could never leave this neighborhood. Lucy Gallivant can have her adventures. My roots are here."

Homer heaved a huge sigh of relief and fell asleep.

Then one morning, Homer had the shock of his life: a sign in his own front yard!

He sniffed it. Just like the one next door! Homer wanted to chase it away. He barked at the sign, but it didn't budge.

Homer found Hank packing books into boxes. Boxes meant moving! Homer whined and yipped and ran circles around Hank's feet.

"Homer!" said Hank. "Behave!"

Hank washed windows and scrubbed the bathtub. "I never thought I'd sell this house," he told Homer. "But this move will be good for us."

Homer tried some of the dog tricks Hank had taught him. He tried to SPEAK to Hank.

"Arf!" (I don't want to move!)

"Woof!" (You promised we'd never move!)

"Grrrrarrrrf!"

Hank said, "Settle down, Homer."

Homer sat up and BEGGED Hank not to move. Hank gave him a treat. "Good trick, Homer."

Homer decided to teach Hank to STAY. He grabbed one of Hank's shoes between his teeth and held on tight.

The doorbell rang. Hank yanked his foot loose. "We have to sell this house before we can buy the new one," he said. "Be quiet, Homer, and don't get in the way."

A man and a woman walked right into Homer's house. The woman wrinkled her nose. "Animals leave a smell in houses," she said.

"It's hard to get rid of," agreed the man.

Hank asked Homer to shake hands with the people. Homer refused. He sat down at their feet and scratched ferociously.

"FLEAS!" the woman shrieked. "That dreadful dog has FLEAS!"

The man piped up, "If there are fleas on the dog, there are fleas all over this house!"

"Millions of fleas!" whined the woman.

They ran from the house, howling and scratching.
Hank said, "Homer, shame on you."

Homer sulked in a kitchen corner while Hank cleaned the oven. Homer chewed on a loose corner of wallpaper. He ripped a strip right off the wall. Then another, and another.

When Hank discovered that, he sent Homer to bed early, without their evening walk.

In the morning, Homer buried one of Hank's shoes in Ms. Gallivant's backyard. That'll teach Hank to STAY, he thought. Hank can't move anywhere with just one shoe.

More people were coming with a real estate agent to look at the house. "This time," said Hank, "no scratching!"

Homer obeyed Hank. He didn't scratch. This time when the people arrived, he hurtled around the house, knocking over lamps and potted plants. He dragged an uprooted philodendron to Hank and shook it, showering everybody with dirt.

"*Rr-r-r-rrts!*" Homer growled.

The people all rushed home to take baths.

Hank said, "Homer, you're spoiling my surprise. I'm fed up with you!"

A few days later, Hank told Homer that somebody else wanted to see the house. "The agent says this is a very interested buyer," said Hank. "I don't want you to ruin the sale. Go to Ms. Gallivant's yard and stay there until they're gone."

Homer wouldn't go. He PLAYED DEAD. Hank had to carry him. He tied Homer to the willow tree.

Alone under the tree, Homer chewed the rope and chewed and chewed until finally he was free.

Homer raced to the Robinsons' yard. *"Arf! Aarf woof grrrrf!"*
"Hey," said Kate. "Homer's upset."
"He's been tied up," said Quinn. "He chewed through this rope."
"We'd better take him to Hank," said Scott.
But just then, the children's mother called them in.

Homer was too mad at Hank to go home. He hid in
the Robinsons' empty garage.
Suddenly the garage door closed. Homer heard the
Robinsons get into their car and drive away. Homer didn't
know they were going on a trip to visit their grandmother
in another state.

For the rest of the day and all the long night, Homer was trapped. He stayed trapped for another day and another night. He got scared and sad and lonely. He found odds and ends of garbage to eat, but with each passing moment, Homer grew sadder and lonelier.

Homer wanted Hank. Not his house, not Ms. Gallivant's yard, but Hank. Was Hank too fed up to look for him?

When the Robinsons finally returned, Homer exploded out the garage door and dashed home.

Moving men were carrying boxes out of his house. Homer didn't care. He hurled himself into Hank's arms and knocked him off his feet.

Hank laughed and cried and hugged Homer. "I was afraid I'd never see you again. I've been searching everywhere."

Homer slathered Hank with sloppy kisses.

Hank said, "I hated the idea of moving without you. But now...
Come on, Homer. I'll show you the surprise...our new house."
And off they went...

…next door to Ms. Gallivant's house!
  "The best house on the block," said Hank.

Homer had never been inside Ms. Gallivant's house before, but he'd always been curious about it. Now he saw Hank's favorite chair in the living room

and his own dish on the kitchen floor.

Homer found his bed next to Hank's.

Homer ran into Ms. Gallivant's yard. His yard now! Homer barked down the rabbit hole. He rolled in the dirt under the willow tree. He raced down the path to the Robinsons' yard and back again.

Homer dug up Hank's shoe and brought it to him.

"Homer," said Hank, "I'm sorry I didn't talk things over with you. Moving is too important to be a surprise."

The next day, Homer and Hank visited their old house. Hank patched the wallpaper in the kitchen. He took down the FOR SALE sign. Then they went home to their new house next door.

And when the new neighbors moved into Homer's old house, who do you suppose they were?

"I'm back! I've had my big adventure. Now I'm ready to settle down," said Lucy Gallivant. "Homer, I want you to meet…

…Gadabout," continued Ms. Gallivant, "my new puppy." Gadabout licked Homer's drool.

"*Woof!*" said Homer.

Isn't life just full of surprises?

Finally, Ms. Gallivant served Homer's favorite biscuits. "You know," she confided to Homer, "I had to come back when I heard your house was for sale. I always thought your house was the best house on the block!"